THIS IGLOO BOOK BELONGS TO:

· ·

igloobooks

Published in 2021
First published in the UK by Igloo Books Ltd
An imprint of Igloo Books Ltd
Cottage Farm, NN6 0BJ, UK
Owned by Bonnier Books
Sveavägen 56, Stockholm, Sweden
www.igloobooks.com

Copyright © 2020 Igloo Books Ltd

0921 002
2 4 6 8 10 9 7 5 3
ISBN 978-1-80022-356-1

Written by Stephanie Moss
Illustrated by Kristen Humphrey

Designed by Alex Alexandrou
Edited by Hannah Campling

Printed and manufactured in China

Magic SQUAD

igloobooks

The Magic Squad is missing!
We don't know where they are.

Will you help me look for them?
They can't have gone too far.

WAIT...

see all that magic dust?

This might be our first clue.

BLOW on it and wish to find them.

Then hope it comes true!

Now that our first missing Magic Squad members are here...

... let's quickly **TURN** the page so that they can't disappear.

Do you see that spooky shadow,
moving on the wall?
It's making funny faces
and I don't like it at all.

Phew! It's only Mermaid in the bath, having a wash.

At least she isn't missing... let's leave her now. SPLISH-SPLOSH!

shhh!

I think I heard a ROAR.

And I can see a snout!

TURN the whole book **upside down**
and then see who *falls* out.

PLONK!

Hi, Little Dragon.

What a lot of noise you make!

(Ruining his nap might have

been quite a big mistake...)

SPIN

the book around
three times.
It might show
us the way.

What,
you've found
some candy?
And it's half
eaten, you say!

The candy made an arrow! And what's it pointing at?

Unicorn is dressing up... and what a funny hat!

We've found the missing Magic Squad.
Well, all except for one.
Where do you think Monster is?
Our search is nearly done...

He isn't in the pantry and he's not under the bed.
He's not up in the attic and he isn't in the shed.

But there, beyond the sandpit,
is a secret little den.

DO NOT ENTER

WIGGLE the book in the
air and see what happens then.

WHOOSH!

You made the wind blow to reveal who's inside...

You finally found Monster.

What a perfect place to hide.

Now you're back together.
You were missing for so long.
We're so glad that we found you
and you're here where you belong.

Wait, don't leave! (Let's call them back.
Shout, "Please, stay here. Don't go!")
We thought that it was just a game.
What is it we don't know?

"We're tired and we need a rest.
We're always fighting crime.
Please **CLAP** your hands and make
us disappear one more time."

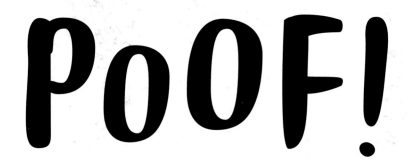

PoOF!

It worked...
they've vanished.
But they won't
always be gone.

If you want to find them,
START the book back at page one.

Until then, close your eyes.
Although it's sad they had to leave,
as the Squad is MAGIC,
they'll come back if you believe!